PRINCESS KHLOE

AND THE TALE OF THE

BADLANDS

By:

RASHEED LATHAM

CHAPTER 1

Once upon a time, there was a beautiful young Princess named Princess Khloe. Princess Khloe grew up in the Badlands where everyone was mean and grumpy all the time, even the animals. Her mother and father kept her hidden away in their castle where she was only allowed out with them because she wasn't like everyone else in her village. That was the reason she didn't mind staying in her room.

People in her village talked mean, looked mean and even walked mean. Princess Khloe on the other hand was totally different from everyone else. She smiled a beautiful smile, said hello and how are you to everyone she walked past. She even walked with a graceful step as if she were floating.

In Princess Khloe's presence you could feel her loving, caring aura which was the reason people acted a little differently toward her. They weren't used to her loving caring ways. When she would go out with her parents the people in the village would stay away from them because of the way Princess Khloe was. The few who did speak only said a few words before taking off leaving Princess Khloe feeling lonely and sad. Because Princess Khloe wasn't like everyone else in her village, she didn't have any friends except for the servants and guards inside of the castle. Her best friend was an older mean maid named Helen who had been inside of the castle for the last thirty eight years and knew every inch of the Badlands.

Helen would tell Princess Khloe about the castle's past but when Princess Khloe would ask certain questions about the outside world, Helen would tell her it was forbidden to talk about.

The Badlands were surrounded by nothing but water and you couldn't see anything else. There was one large boat on their land but only her father and other crew members were allowed on board. The boat only went out twice a year and that was to the middle of the ocean to fish for the next six months.

Legend has it that there were other people in the world…other people that were nothing like the people of the Badlands. Rumor has it that there are other people out there like Princess Khloe. That's why she was so intrigued by the old stories Helen would tell her and asked the question she did…questions that were forbidden to be answered.

CHAPTER 2

Today, Princess Khloe was sitting at her desk in front of her large mirror thinking about tomorrow. Tomorrow was her 17th birthday and she had no idea what her family had planned for her. Last year she had a birthday party and only nine people showed up and they were the people that stayed inside the castle. She hoped her party wasn't like that this year because it would really hurt her feelings.

"Princess Khloe, it's time to eat lunch," Ms.Helen said in a low raspy voice with a mean look on her face.
"Good afternoon Ms.Helen,"
"Yeah yeah," Ms.Helen said as she began cleaning Princess Khloe's room. She was throwing things into the drawers and closet knocking other things over but she didn't care.
"Ms.Helen, my birthday is tomorrow. Did you remember?" Princess Khloe asked getting up from her desk. As usual she was wearing a big bright smile.
"No," Ms.Helen said walking right past Princess Khloe like she was invisible.

"Ms.Helen," Princess khloe said in a low voice as she fell against her bed.

"What?" Ms.Helen said turning toward Princess Khloe with the same mean look she had on her face as before. Ms.Helen had a long nose that used to scare Princess Khloe when she was little. Now that she was older it made Princess Khloe laugh.

"I'm scared that people aren't going to come to my party like they did last year because I'm not like other people," Princess Khloe said pouting.

"Well, be like other people," Ms.Helen told Princess Khloe before leaving her room.

When Ms.Helen left Princess Khloes's room, Princess Khloe went back to her mirror to think about what Ms.Helen had said.

"Be like other people," Princess Khloe said into the mirror with a smile on her face before twisting it up into a wicked grin. Princess Khloe wasn't like the other people in her village but if she wanted her party to be a success she knew that's what she had to do.

When Princess Khloe made it down stairs to the dinner table her parents were there waiting on her.

"Good afternoon mother, father," Princess Khloe said as she sat down at the table.

Even though her parents were used to the way Princess Khloe acted they still didn't like it one bit.

"Princess," her father said as he placed a napkin on his lap. "Princess Khloe wipe that silly smirk off of your face," her mother yell.

"What smirk mom?" Princess Khloe asked knowing what her mother was talking about but she couldn't help it.

"That ridiculous smile that you keep on your face," her mother told her.

"I can't help it mother. Besides, I don't think I would like my face to be frowned up all day," Princess Khloe told them as she began to play with her silverware.

"Even if you don't like it,you will have to get used to it Princess. One day you will be the Queen of the Badlands and people will have to fear you. How could someone fear you and you're standing on the throne with that silly smirk on your face," her father yelled with his face twisted up.

"Your father is right Princess. One day you will be the queen of the Badlands and people will never respect you if you still have that silly smirk by the time that time comes," her mother said as she began to eat her food.

Princess Khloe sat at the table still playing with her silverware. The smile she always wore was now gone. What her mother said about her becoming the Princess one day and the people of the Badlands not respecting her really hurt her feelings.

***

After sitting at the table quietly and doing nothing, Princess Khloe was allowed to go to her room where she was now sitting in her mirror. What her parents and Ms.Helen had said to her was still on her mind. Princes Khloe didn't want to be a Princess that wasn't respected and also didn't want her party to turn out like it had last year.

"If I want to be the Queen of the Badlands one day I will have to wipe this silly smirk off of my face," Princess Khloe said looking into the mirror with her loving, caring smile but within seconds the beautiful smile Princess Khloe always wore on her cute little face was now gone. Her face was now twisted up like she knew her parents and the people of the Badlands would love.

CHAPTER 3

The next day Princess Khloe woke up with a smile on her face realizing what day it was. Today was her birthday and she was excited. That is until she remembered what she had to do today. Princess Khloe wanted her birthday party to be a success and for that to happen she had to be like the other people of the Badlands.

Princess Khloe twisted her face into the meanest face she could muster but it wasn't much. Princess Khloe had never twisted her face up or thought about being mean to anyone so today was going to be hard for her.

She threw her covers to the floor and got out of bed to look at herself in the mirror. Seeing herself with her face twisted up like that made her fall out laughing until she heard someone knock at her door. She jumped up off of the floor and twisted her face back up. She wasn't going to let a silly smirk mess up another one of her birthdays.

"Come in!" She yelled like she never had before. Ms. Helen walked into the room and instantly looked at the floor. She was surprised to see Princess Khloe's covers on the floor. For the last ten years Princess Khloe had been making her bed and keeping her room clean as a whistle before anyone could step inside. Today was something that Ms. Helen had never seen and she liked it. Even though she would have to make Princess Khloe's bed now.

"Princess Khloe, why is your bed not made?" Ms. Helen asked finally turning to Princess Khloe. That's when she saw the evil smirk on Princess Khloes face.

"Because i'm not making it!" The Princess yelled as she went and sat in front of her large mirror.

"Yes Princess, be mean," Ms. Helen said rubbing her hands together.

"Hush Ms. Helen and clean," the Princess said as she began to brush her hair.

"Yes Princess," Ms. Helen said as she began to clean Princess Khloe's room. Once she was done cleaning, Ms. Helen ran out of Princess Khloe's room to spread the wonderful news about how Princess Khloe made her clean her room and yelled at her with her face twisted up. Princess Khloe laughed because she knew that's exactly what Ms. Helen was going to do.

Once the Princess finished bathing and brushing her teeth she went downstairs where her parents were waiting on her to start breakfast. When she entered the room both of her parents were staring at her with weird looks on their faces.

"Stop looking at me like that!" Princess Khloe yelled catching them off guard. The king and Queen looked at each other with shocked looks on their faces. The couldn't believe the Princess had yelled at them for the first time in her life. They were so proud of her.

"Yes Princess." Her father said before he began to eat his food. Her mother was still staring at the Princess amazed. "It's your birthday is it?" Mr.Gregory asked walking into the kitchen.

"Oh hush up Gregory," The princess said stopping him in his tracks.

"Oh my, it's true. The Princess can be mean!" He yelled before running back out of the kitchen. He was going to spread the word just like Ms. Helen had.

After breakfast, Princess Khloe went back to her room to get ready for her big day. Once inside her room she could hear people talking outside her window. She curiously went over to the window and took a look outside. Ms. Helen and Mr. Gregory spreading the word about her being mean must have spread fast because there were at least 50 outside of the castle wall looking up at her window.

"Look, there she is," a man yelled. Princess Khloe moved back away from the window because she could feel that silly smirk coming across her face and she couldn't have that right now. These people were here for her birthday and she wasn't going to run them off with a stupid smile. She twisted her face back up and went back to the window.

"What do you people want?" She yelled. The village people's eyes got big and they began to whisper to one another. "What do you people want?" She yelled again when no one answered her.

"Today is your birthday!" The same man yelled. "Yeah, so," she said shrugging her shoulders.

"What time is the party?" A girl around the same age as the Princess asked.

"Yeah, what time is the party?" another girl around the same age as the Princess asked. The Princess had to control herself because she was ready to smile at any second. She hadn't talked to girls her age who actually seemed to like her in forever.

"The party is at whatever time the party is. Just make sure you all are there!" The Princess yelled before slamming her window and walking away from it. She could still hear people talking outside of her window. Inside her room alone, she began to smile happy that she was finally going to have a regular birthday party for the first time in her life.

CHAPTER 4

Princess Khloe and her parents made their way to the courtyard with their guards behind them. The courtyard was where Princess Khloe's party was being held and she was anxious to see how things had turned out after what happened at her window. Once the doors to the courtyard opened the frown on Princess Khloe's face was almost replaced with a silly smirk but she couldn't let that happen. There were hundreds of people inside of the courtyard waiting to see Princess Khloe for her birthday and she couldn't believe it.

"The Princess is here!" A woman yelled letting everyone know the Princess had arrived. Everyone had their faces twisted up but the Princess could tell they were happy to see the new her.

"Hush! It's my birthday not yours!" The Princess yelled.

"Yes Princess!" A man yelled as he hushed the people of the Badlands. Princess Khloe was led to the throne with her parents. The three of them had their faces twisted up into the meanest grins. Once they were at the throne, Princess Khloe stood and grabbed the microphone.

"Why are you all here?" The Princess asked as she looked around at the huge crowd.

"It's your birthday Princess and we came here to celebrate with you," a man yelled from the crowd.

"It's about time you people finally got some sense! I am the Princess and you all will learn to respect me!" The Princess yelled while looking at all the village people.

"Yes Princess yes!" The village people chanted loving the new mean Princess.

The party begins and everyone begins to enjoy their mean selves. Everyone except for Princess Khloe. Even though the Princess agreed to be mean for the sake of her party, she still couldn't find herself to be mean as everyone else. The way people were treating each other was so mean and the Princess couldn't take it anymore.

When no one was watching her, Princess Khloe left out the back of the courtyard and went into the woods. The woods were nowhere for the Princess to be but she just needed to get away from everybody. The Princess held her mean face up for as long as she could but being mean wasn't her.

She roamed through the forest crying until she came to the ocean. The Princess had only seen the ocean twice in her life and that was with her parents. She began to look out into the water wishing she was in a better place. A place where people didn't act like the people of the Badlands.

The Princess fell to her knees still crying. That is until she heard a noise that was unfamiliar to her. The Princess looked up and was surprised at what she saw and heard.

"Hey, what's this?/ this shouldn't even exist/ hey that's land, that wasn't in my plans/ I...am stran, stranddy addy ann," a boy around the same age as Princess Khloe said as he let his boat sail onto land. The way he connected his words together intrigued the Princess. Instead of running away scared, the Princess hid behind a large tree and continued to watch him.

The Princess had never seen the young man before but knew he wasn't from the Badlands. She knew because she had never seen him before plus the way he was talking and the big smile he had on his face even though he was stranded gave it away.

The young man stepped off on his small boat and began to look around the large wooden area.

"Hello…anyone out there?" He yelled. When no one answered him his smile faded into a sad look. "Oh, what am I going to do now?" He asked himself as he began to kick rocks around. He kicked his third rock over to where the Princess was hiding and for some reason he liked the color of the small rock. He went over to pick the rock up to put on his boat so he could take home with him, whenever he got his boat fixed.

"Whoaa...who are you?" He asked stumbling back once he saw the Princess standing there with her face twisted up into the meanest face.

"Ha ha ha, and why are you standing there with that silly smirk on your face?" He asked laughing and smiling again.

This was the first person the Princess had ever seen laugh and smile and she was so excited but she couldn't let her guard down that easily.

"I am Princess Khloe of the Badlands and you are trespassing mister!" The Princess yelled.

"I'm Ken," he said while looking her over. "Princess yeah. Of the BadLands, I don't think so. If you were the Princess of the Badlands you would have been called your troops and had me thrown back into the ocean," he told her.

When Ken said that, the Princess began to look down at the ground. What he said was true or at least should have been. Her parents would have been had Ken thrown into the dungeon but the Princess wasn't like her parents.

"The truth is, I am the Princess of the Badlands but i'm not like everyone else in my village. I'm different," she told him.

"What do you mean you're not like everyone else?" Ken asked sounding concerned. "Oh, do you mean that silly face when I first saw you?" He asked laughing.

"Yes. Everyone of the Badlands is mean and I am nothing like them," she said as she began to kick around rocks on the ground. "I like to smile, laugh and be happy. Like you were when I first saw you. You were smiling and talking. Well you weren't talking. You were doing something with your voice that sounded nice," the Princess said finally looking up at him.

"What do you mean singing?" He asked with a confused look on his face.

"Is that what you call it? We don't make our voices sound like that here in the Bad Land," the Princess told him.

"You guys don't sing here? Oh my, you guys are mean. Singing makes you happy like a breath of fresh air," he said jumping onto a big rock with a big smile on his face. "Today, today…was not a good day/ my boat…my boat , my boat took me astray/ astray astray please not today/" He sang until his smile turned into a sad frown.

"What's wrong?" The Princess asked know sounding concerned as Ken had.

"Today is the town festival and I was supposed to deliver the fish but unfortunately my boat took a hit causing it to flood. I had to stop and this was the first piece of land I saw," he said with a sad look on his face.

The Princess could tell he was sad and didn't like it. "I can help," she told him.

"Why would the Princess of the Badlands help little ole me?" Ken asked.

"Because I'm not like everyone else in the Badlands. Besides, where are you from?" The Princess asked.

"Me…I'm from a place where the sun shines even when it's night. The people are friendly and say good morning. The flowers are fresh and even the mice are nice. I'm from the Happy Lands," Ken said with a big smile on his face.

"Tell me more about the Happy Lands," the Princess said excitedly to hear about happy people. She had heard old stories about the Happy Lands but didn't think they were true.

"The Happy Lands are nothing like the Badlands. We are always happy even if we're sad. That's the good thing about everything. I love it there," he told her still smiling.

"I want to go to the Happy Lands," the Princess said picturing herself in a land of happy people. People like her.

"You want to leave the Badlands?" He asked standing next to her.

"I don't but I don't feel like myself here. I want to be happy and smile all day like the people of the Happy Lands. I think I would be so happy there. Will you take me?" She asked excitedly.

"I don't know about that Princess. What will your parents think?" He asked.

"They want know. I'll help you get your boat fixed if you promise to take me to the Happy Lands and bring me back," the Princess told him.

Ken sat there thinking for a couple seconds. "Are you sure Princess?" Ken asked.

"Yes. As long as I'm back in time, my parents won't know anything." the Princess told him.

Ken sat there for a couple seconds thinking. "Ok Princess, only if I can make it back in time for the festival. The people of the village are depending on me." Ken said with a sad look on his face.

The Princess didn't like him looking like that when she knew he was from the Happy Lands and should be smiling. "Deal." the Princess said smiling.

"I'll be back." the Princess said walking off.

***

Back at the courtyard, the Princess found Ms. Helen who she told about Ken and promised her not to tell anyone but the people who would help her. Ms. Helen gathered up two guards and followed the Princess to where Ken was.

Ms. Helen and the guards helped Ken fix his boat and was happy to see him leave until the Princess told them she was going with him.

"What do you mean you're leaving Princess?" Ms. Helen asked with her face twisted up more than it had ever been before.

"Ms. Helen, I'm not happy here. I want to see the Happy Lands. I want to see other people like me," the Princess said with tears falling from her eyes.

Ms. Helen had never felt a sad feeling in her life but at that moment she felt sad. She had known the Princess all her life and knew that she was different from everyone else in the Badlands. She wanted the Princess to be happy and she knew that wouldn't happen on the Badlands.

"I promise Ms. Helen. I'll be back before bedtime," the Princess said with the saddest look on her face.

"Ok Princess but make sure you're back in time for bed!" Ms.Helen yelled.

"I promise Ms. Helen. Come on Ken. It's time to go," the Princess said excitedly. She couldn't wait to see the Happy Lands.

"See you folks later," Ken said waving to Ms. Helen and the two guards that were with her. Ms. Helen or the guard said anything to Ken. Instead they all just stared at him with their faces twisted but he knew what that meant. Even if they wanted to be nice, they couldn't.

Ken and the Princess sailed off into the ocean with smiles on their faces. For the first time in her life the Princess was around someone who appreciated her smile.

CHAPTER 5

It had been a long trip and by the time they made it to the Happy Lands Princess Khloe was sound asleep. Ken had sung songs the whole way there and the Princess loved every minute of it which was the reason she was asleep.

"Princess Khloe, we're here," Ken said grabbing her by her hand and waking her out of her sleep.

When the Princess woke up she couldn't believe her eyes. Everything was so beautiful. The trees, the birds, the grass and even the water.

"Come on Princess, we have to walk for a distance," Ken said helping her from the boat. He then grabbed the net he had stored the town's fish in before him and the Princess made their way through the forest.

"Staring into your eyes I see.../ the perfect place for meeee/ look one time and you will seeee/ there's no one else but meeee/" Ken sang as they made their way through the forest. Ken's voice was something she wasn't used to but she loved it. If she would have closed her eyes, she would have still been able to follow his lovely voice.

"Where here," Ken said as he pulled a large leaf back. Soon as he did, music instantly began to play.

"Oh my," the Princess said covering her mouth. The festival had started and there were people everywhere.

The Princess began to smile and laugh

because everyone else was.

"Ken's back," a kid yelled before running over to where Ken and the Princess were.

"Hey Arthur," Ken said rubbing the kid's head.

"Who's this?" The kid asked looking at Princess Khloe. "This here is Princess Khloe. She's from…" Ken paused before looking at Khloe. "She's from the Sad Lands," Ken lied, which was against the rules of the Happy Lands. The thing is, the people of the Happy Lands didn't speak or think of people of the Badlands. So for Ken to bring Princess Khloe to the Happy Lands was really against the rules. Even though it was against the rules, Ken had seen Princess Khloe wasn't like the people of the Badlands. That was the reason he decided to go against the rules for her.

When Ken lied to Authur, the Princess was about to say something until Authur grabbed her other hand and began to pull her away from Ken.

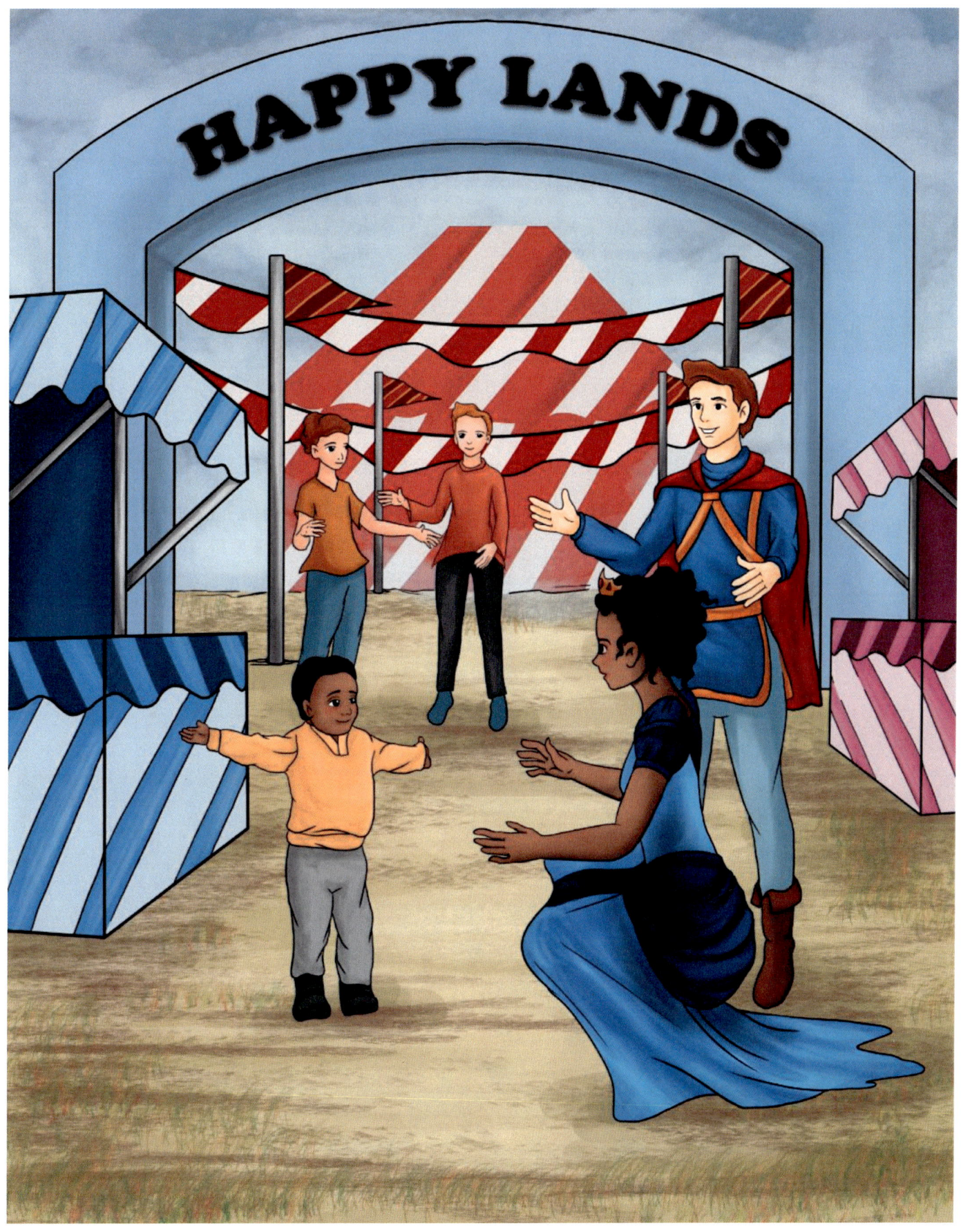

"Come on Princess. This is the Happy Lands and there's no reason to be sad here. Today is the big festival and we're going to have so much fun." Arthur said excitedly as he led her into the crowd of people.

The Princess was greeted by everyone with open arms and smiles. Everyone was happy to meet her and she was happy to be there. Even though she was happy to be there she wished her family was there to be happy with her.

"Princess Khloe, how do you like the Happy Lands so far?" Ken asked as he handed her a cup. "I love it here," The Princess said with a big smile on her face. "I love the people, the colors and I really love the singing." She said before spinning in a circle. When she stopped, she took a sip from her cup. "Oh my, this is delicious. What is it?" She asked before taking another sip from her cup.

"That's our famous Happy Land juice. We only make it during the four festivals of the year." he said as they walked off from Authur and his friends who had shown the Princess their best dance moves.

"You guys have four of these a year?" Princess asked still looking around at all the activities that were going on. The best party in the Badlands couldn't compare to what she was seeing.

"Yeah but we have parties every weekend unless it's somebody's birthday, a baby is born, a celebration is caused for for if someone is just really really happy which is always," he said laughing. "Come on Princess, I want you to meet my parents." He said grabbing her hand and pulling her away from the kids.

When the Princess and Ken stepped in front of his parents the Princess couldn't believe what she was seeing. Ken's parents were sitting on the throne just like her parents were back in the BadLands, which meant they were a King and queen and Ken was a Prince.

"Mother, father, I would like you to meet Princess Khloe of the Sad Lands," Ken told his parents. Their bright smiles instantly faded and they looked at each other before looking back at the Prince and Princess.

Ken had a shocked look on his face which he never had before. He was looking shocked because he had never seen his parents without a smile on their faces.

They even smiled when they were sleeping. The Prince was lost for words and the Princess was standing there wondering why their moods had changed the way they had.

"Hi Princess Khloe. Welcome to the Happy Lands" the king said smiling again.

"Yes, welcome Princess Khloe. It's nice to finally meet you," the Queen said smiling again.

When she said that Khloe began to look confused wondering what the Queen meant when she said it was nice to finally meet her. How did the Queen know about Princess Khloe when everyone thinks their Lands are the only ones in the world. The Princess couldn't take it anymore and had to ask.

"Excuse me Queen, what did you mean when you said it's nice to finally meet me? You've heard of me before, but how?" The Princess asked.

The Queen looked over at the King who nodded his head while holding her hand. The Queen turned back toward the Princess ready to tell her why her parents and the adults of the Badlands had been keeping everyone else in the world a secret. Before the Queen could say anything they heard someone call the Princess name. When she looked behind her, her father (the King of the Badlands) was standing behind her and had over fifty guards standing behind him. Including the one that helped Ken fix his boat.

"Princess Khloe, what are you doing out of the Badlands and here with these people!" Her father yelled at the top of his lungs causing his chest to heave up and down.

"Father, what are you doing here?" The princess asked her father the same question he had asked her which only made him madder.

"Princess you know you are not to leave the Badlands, it is forbidden!" He yelled.

"Why father, why? Why is the Happy Lands forbidden? Please tell me father, please." The princess begged with tears falling from her eyes. In the short time Princess Khloe had been in the Happy Lands she had fallen in love with the place and knew deep down in her heart that that's where she belonged. She wasn't like the people back in the Badlands and everyone could see that. There in Happy Land she was like everyone and loved it which was the reason she wanted to know why it was forbidden to go to, talk about or even know about the Happy Lands.

"Yes King, tell her why it's forbidden for her to visit the happiest place in the world." The King of the Happy Lands told the King of the Badlands.

"You stay out of this. And you." The King of the Bad Land said before pointing at Ken. "If you ever trespass on the Badlands again I will have you thrown into the dungeon for the next fifty years for violating the treaty between our lands. Let's go Princess!" The King yelled stepping to the side which caused his guards to form a path for the Princess to walk through.

The Princess wanted to say something but she couldn't because her tears wouldn't stop falling. She turned to say goodbye to Ken and to thank him for giving her the best

birthday present ever by bringing her to the Happy Lands.
"Let's go Princess, now!" Her father yelled.

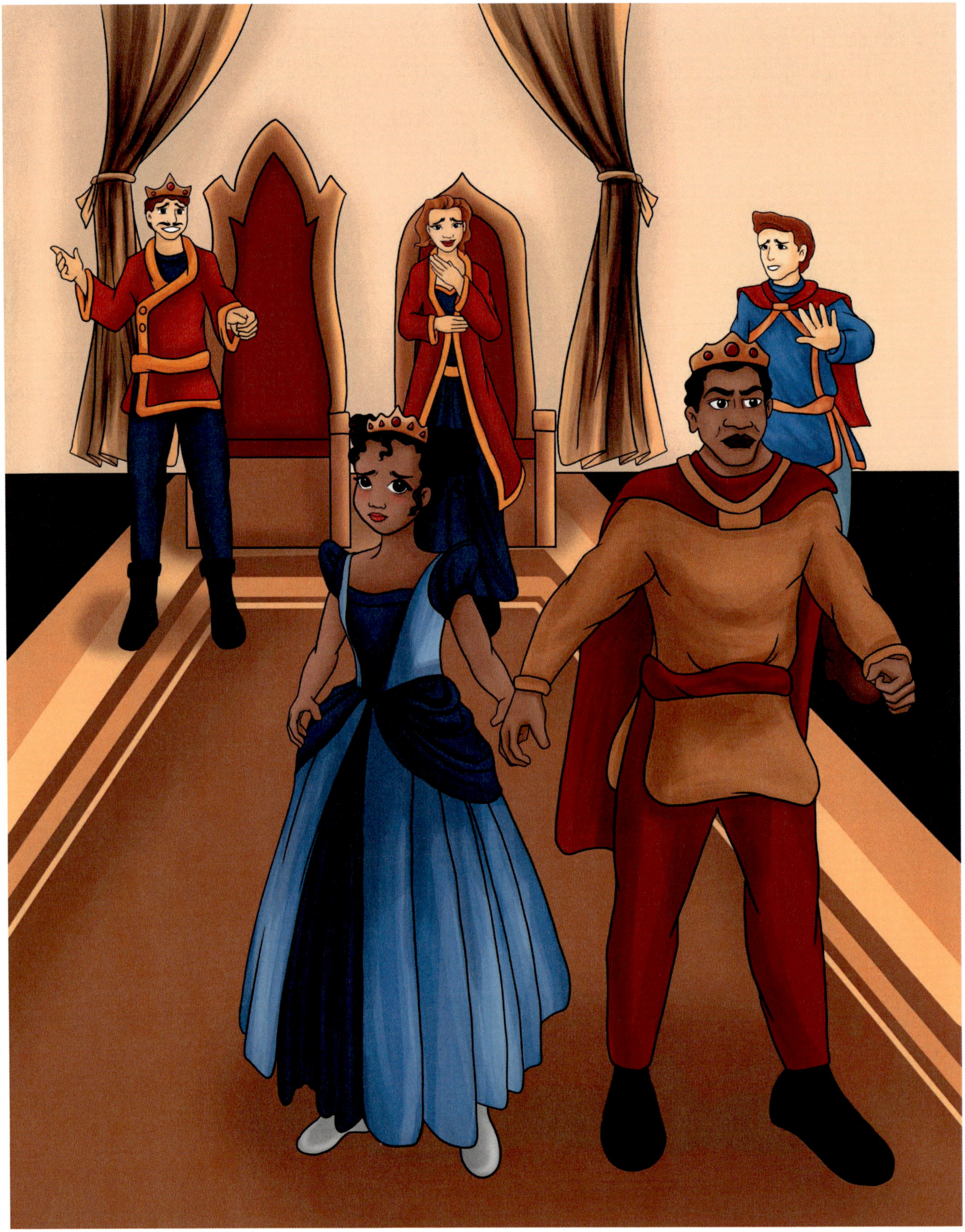

"Bye Ken." She said wiping tears from her eyes before walking away from Ken. The person she only knew for a few hours but felt like she had known her whole life. "Bye Princess. She heard him say softly as walked away. Once she began to walk through the path of her father's guards she looked back over her shoulder and saw Ken wiping tears from his eyes. "This isn't right father!" She yelled still crying before she took off running to their boat.

CHAPTER 6

It had been a month since the Princess had been to the Happy Lands but it only felt like yesterday to her. All throughout the day the Princess would relive the day she had met Prince Ken to keep the memory fresh because she never wanted to forget about him or the great time he showed her. After that day the Princess stayed in her room more than ever. She felt like she was in her own personal prison and it was starting to get to her. Once she saw how the people on the Happy Lands lived she knew that that's where she belonged but the treaty between the lands wouldn't allow that. She still hadn't figured out why the treaty was set and that too was bothering her. The treaty that was set years ago between the two lands was causing the Princess her happiness so she had to get to the bottom of it but where did she start?

"Ms.Helen." She said with her face twisted up. If anybody was going to tell her what was going on it was Ms.Helen. Just as the Princess got up from her bed someone knocked at her door before walking into her room.

"Khloe why are you still laying in that bed with that awful sad look on your face? This is not the Sad Lands.

You're such a confused child." Her mother said shaking her head.

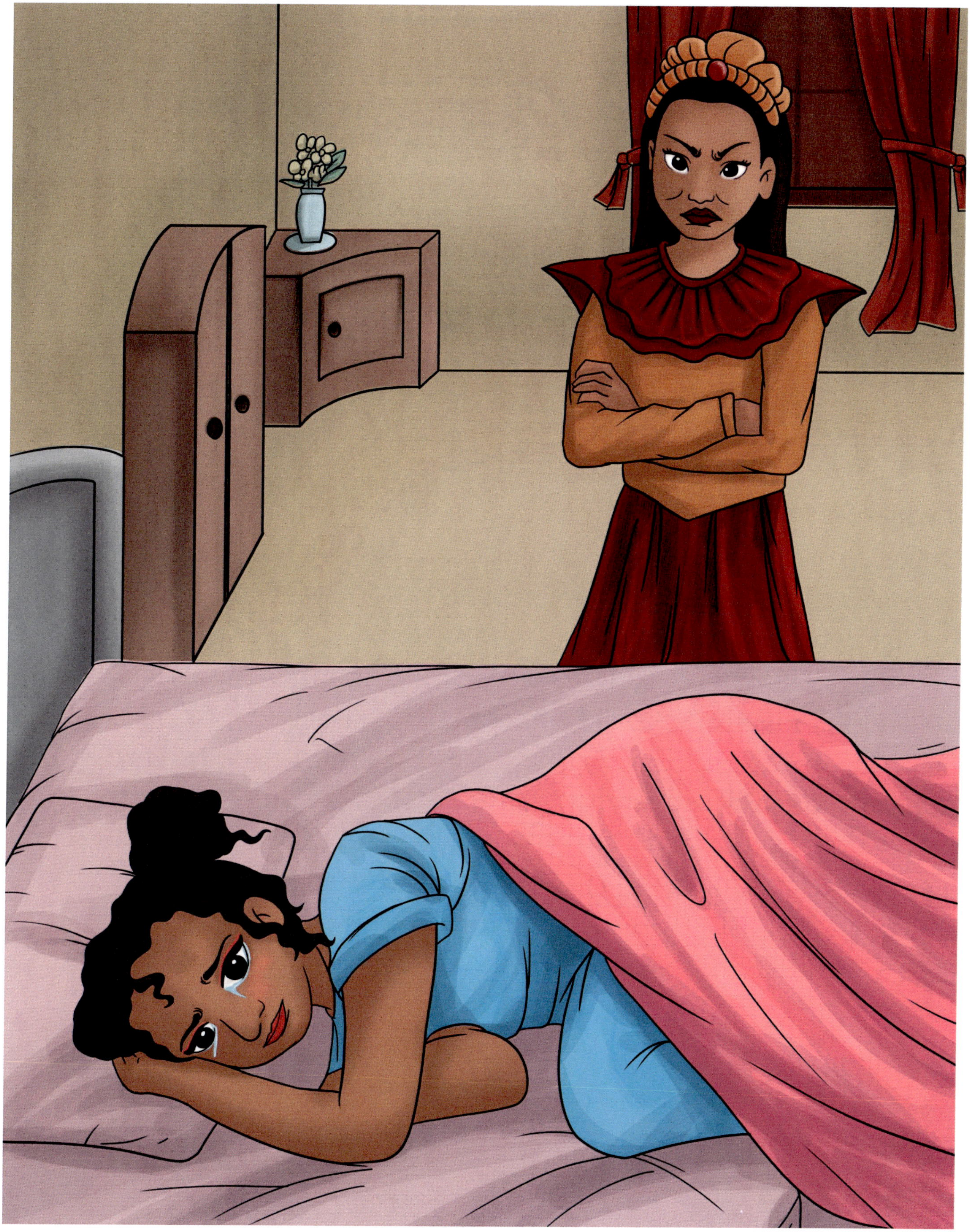

"I'm not confused mother. I know where I want to be and it's not here. Why want he just let me leave to be happy? I'm not happy here." The Princess said with tear filled eyes.

"Because it's forbidden Khloe. Your father didn't make the rules nor will he break or ignore them. There are a lot of bad people out there and he's only trying to protect you. Maybe one day things will change but until then you will forget you ever left the Badlands and anything that came after it. Including that boy. Now get ready to come down for supper." Her mother said before leaving the Princess's room.

"The only bad people in the world are the people that's here in the Badlands. I have to find Ms.Helen and find out what's going on. I can't forget about Ken, because I know he's not going to forget about me." The Princess said before leaving out of her room. She made her way to Ms.Helen's room with her face twisted up ready to get to the bottom of things.

"Ms.Helen!" The Princess yelled bursting into Ms.Helen's room. Ms.Helen looked up at the Princess with a shocked look on her face. "I am the Princess of the Badlands and I demand you tell me what's going on or I will have you thrown into the dungeon for the next thirty years for lying!" The Princess yelled. Ms.Helen sat there for a couple seconds before the Princess saw the corner of Ms.Helen's lips begin to curl up into a smile but for only a second.

PRINCESS KHLOE

"Well Princess, it's about time you came around. Shut the door and pull up a chair because this is a long story." Ms.Helen said before laying back in her bed. "It all started over fifty years ago. There were two Kings who despised each other...one of them was your great grandfather." Ms.Helen told the Princess with a wicked look on her face.

After sitting and talking with Ms.Helen for an hour. The Princess finally knew why her parents and the people of the Badlands acted like no one else existed but she couldn't let that stand between her happinest. The Princess made her way back to her room to figure out a plan but a familiar sound stopped her in her tracks.

"Where is that coming from?" The Princess asked herself as she made her way up the hallway toward the noise she was hearing. When she got to Mr.Trevor's room she stopped and put her ear up against his door. A smile instantly came across her face when she heard Mr.Trevor singing in a low tone. After a few seconds of listening she stepped back away from the door with her face twisted up. The song he was singing was familiar to and the Princess only heard singing in one place, the Happy Lands.

"How does Mr.Trevor know that song?" The Princess asked herself while still staring at his door with her face twisted up. As he continued to sing the Princess burst into his room.

"Princess." Mr.Trevor said startled as he backed against his room wall. The scared look he had on his face told the Princess he was going to tell her exactly what she needed to know.

"How do you know how to sing and how do you know that song? I demand you tell me now before I have you locked away!" The Princess yelled. The Princess had been threatening to throw people in the dungeon and locking them up but deep down in her heart she knew she couldn't hurt anyone by throwing them in a place like that.

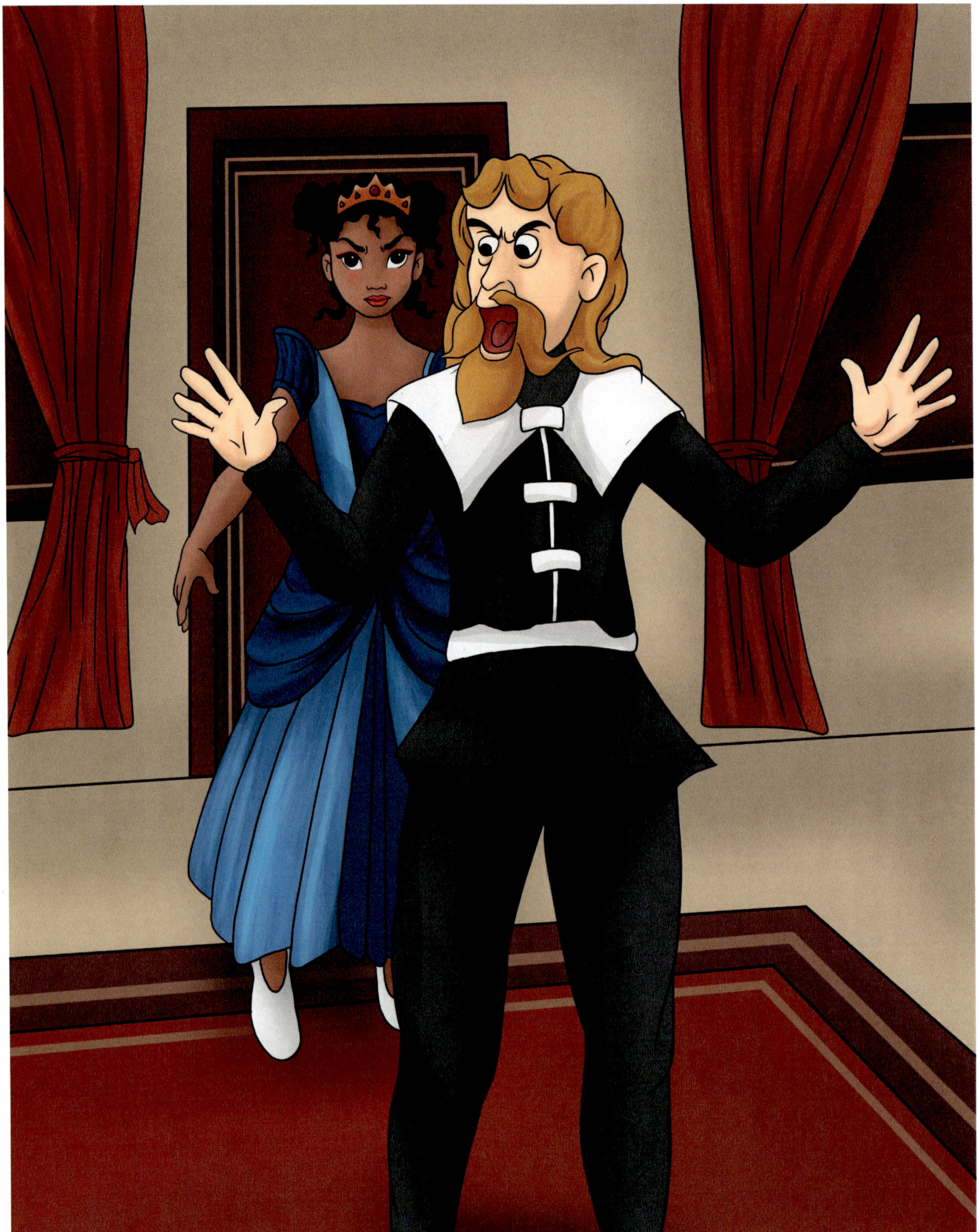

"I'm sorry Princess, it will never happen again. Please don't lock me away, please." He begged before falling to his knees at her feet.

"Mr.Trevor, I want lock you away as long as you tell me what I need to know, I promise. Now how do you know how to sing?" She asked as she helped him up from the floor.

Mr.Trevor went to his door and looked out into the hallway suspiciously before shutting the door. He then looked down at the ground for a few seconds before looking back up at the Princess.

"Please Princess, you mustn't tell anyone I'm telling you this. It's been a secret for the last few weeks and must stay that way." He told her anxiously as he began to pace the floor.

"I promise I want tell anyone Mr.Trevor. Please tell me what's going on." The Princess said softly.

"There's a strange boy locked away in the dungeon and he keeps…" Mr.Trevor plaused before looking away from the Princess.

"He keeps what Mr.Trevor?" The Princess asked seeing Mr.Trevor become afraid of talking any more.

"Princess, I learned singing from the strange boy and for some reason he keeps asking about you." He told her.

When he said that the Princess began to shake her head as tears fell from her eyes.

"What do you mean he's locked away in the dungeon?" She asked wiping her tears.

"Yes. The guards caught the strange kid sneaking around the castle and the king had him immediately thrown into the dungeon. We have no idea where the strange kid came from or what he wants but the King says we must keep it a secret, especially from you. So please, you must keep this between us." He told her.

"Oh I will." She said before leaving his room.
The Princess knew the strange kid Mr.Trevor was talking about being locked in the dungeon was Ken and she had to get him out of there but how?

CHAPTER 7

The next day the Princess woke up bright and early. She had to if she wanted her plan to work. She went to the dining room where she knew Ms.Halan was preparing breakfast.The Princess sat at the head of the table, crossed her arms, twisted her face up and waited on Ms.Helen to come and set the table.

"Princess, what are you doing up this early?" Ms. Helen asked once she entered the dining room.

"I need to go to the dungeon." The Princess said sternly causing Ms.Helen to stop in her tracks.

"The dungeon, what in the world do you want to go there for?" Ms. Helan asked confused because nobody wanted to go to the dungeon voluntarily.

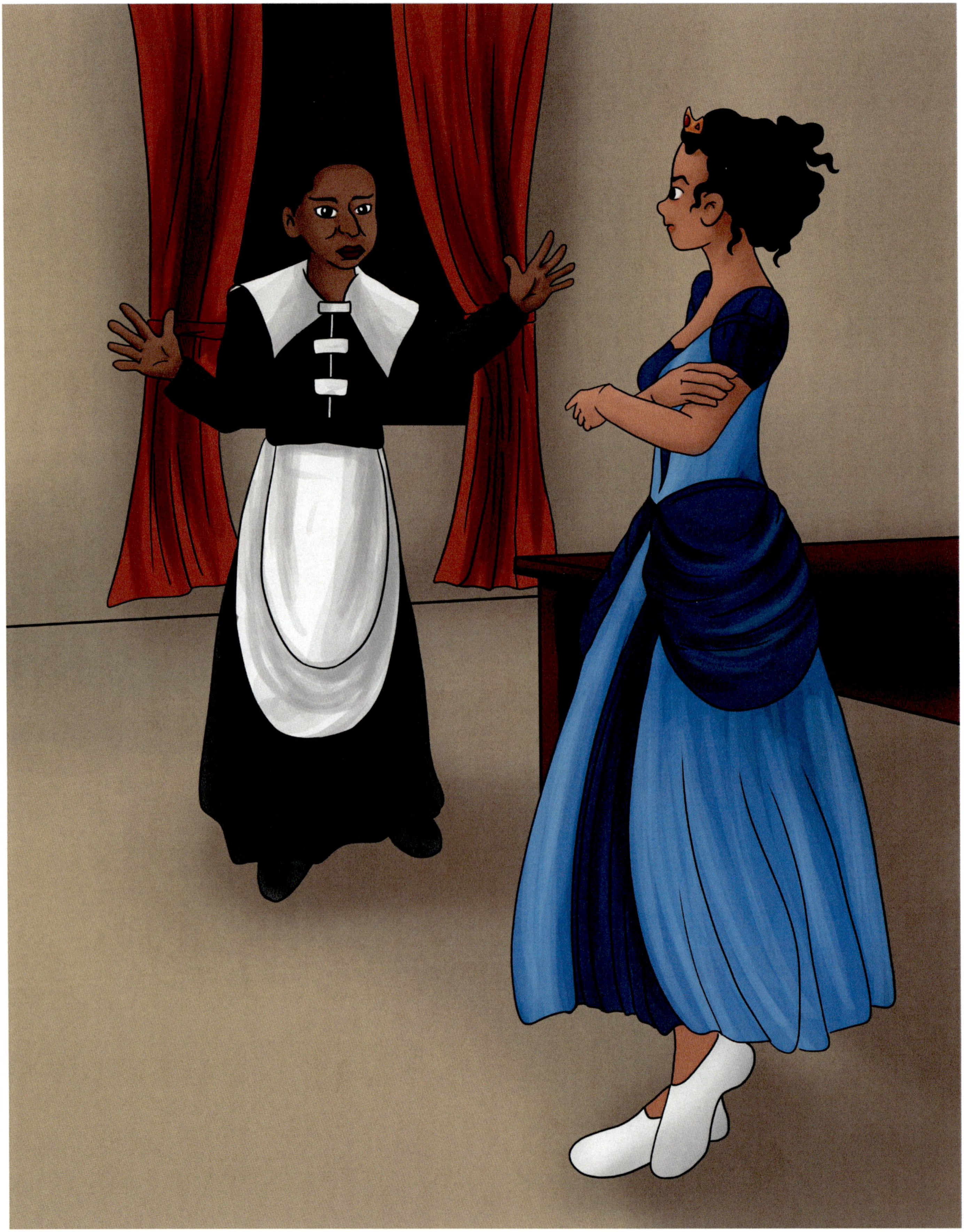

"I have to see him. He's here because of me." The Princess said with tears in her eyes. She had been crying ever since she found out about Ken being locked away in the dungeon.

"See who Princess?" Ms.Helen asked now with a concerned look on her face after seeing the sad look on the Princess's face.

"You don't know?"

"Know what Princess? Ms.Helen asked before sitting at the table with the Princess. The look on Ms.Harlan's face told the Princess she didn't know about Ken being locked away in the dungeon. Even though Ms.Helen was from the Badlands the Princess could tell that she liked Ken. Who wouldn't like Ken? He's kind, giving, polite, charming and not to mention handsome.

"My father has Ken locked up in the dungeon and I need to see him."

"I had no idea Princess. I'm sorry but if that boy came back here he deserves to be locked up."

"But he came back for me. That has to be the reason he's here and I have to see him." The Princess said with tears in her eyes. "I know you can take me to the dungeon through the secret passage. Please Ms.Helen, I need to see him." The Princess begs.

Ms.Helen sat looking at the Princess because what she was asking was against the rules and would get her thrown into the dungeon."Ok Princess, i'll take you to see him but you must not tell anyone." She said with a serious look on her face.

"Thank you so much Ms.Helen and I promise I won't tell anyone about this."

"I will come to your room later on tonight to take you to see him."

"Thank you so much Ms.Helen." the Princess

said before leaving the dining room.

That night the Princess couldn't sleep because she was so happy about seeing Ken again. Around three in the morning Ms.Helen went into the Princess's room, the Princess was wide awake.

"Is it time?" The Princess asked

"Yes it is. Please come Princess and be very quiet." They left the Princess's room and made their way to the old passage through the old passage that leads to the dungeon. Once they made it down to the dungeon they heard singing. The Princess ran up the hall until she found where the singing was coming from. She stopped when she saw Ken laying down on a dirty rug.

"Ken."The Princess whispered through the bars.

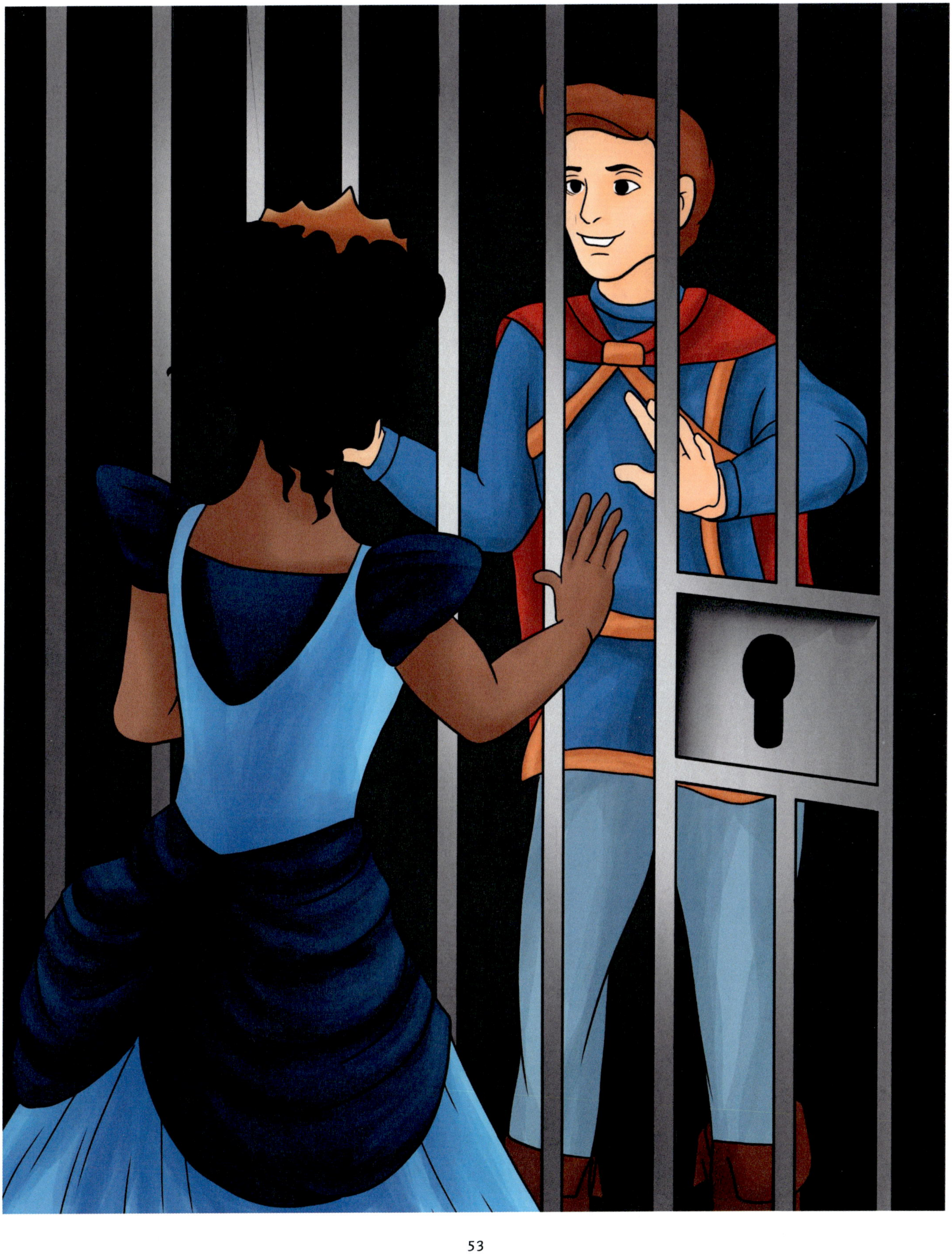

"Princess Khloe what are you doing here, you shouldn't be here." He asked sounding concerned for her even though he was the one locked in the dungeon.

"I came when I heard someone was down in the dungeon singing. I knew it had to be you. When did you come back?" she asked but he put his head down. "Why Ken, why did you come back?"

"Because I just had to see you again Princess. I know you don't belong here and that you are not happy here. With me in the Happy Lands is where you belong but when I tried to explain that to your father he threw me into the dungeon and said I will never take his daughter like my great great grandfather had. I have no idea what that meant but he was sure mad." Ken said laughing. Even though he was in the dungeon Ken was still the happy person he was born to be.

"I know what it means but you're right, I don't belong here and neither do you. Im getting you out of here."

The Princess walked away from Ken and up to Ms.Helen and demanded that she gather up a couple's servants and a boat because her and Ken were leaving the Badlands for good.

Because Princess Khloe was the Princess Ms.Helen did as she was told. With-in an hour Ken was out of the dungeon and him and Princess Khloe were sailing across the ocean to the Happy Lands.

CHAPTER 8

"Princess Khloe, it's nice to see you again after your father took you away like that." The Queen of the Happy Lands said once she saw Ken and the Princess walking up to their castle. "And Ken the whole town has been worried sick about you but I see where you ran off too." The Queen says with a beautiful smile.

"I knew that's where you were going. Young love is something you can't fight." The King said before walking up and giving Princess Khloe and Ken both hugs.

"Yes it is but young love is the reason the lands are divided as they are now." The Queen told them.

"I know the story of what happened between our families but maybe things can change because there is no way I'm going back to that place." The Princess told the Queen.

"Well Princess you will always have a home here in the Happy Lands but what do you think your parents will think about that?" The Queen asked.

"My parents don't care about anyone but the people of the Badlands being the meanest people on earth. If they cared about me they would let me stay here in the Happy Lands instead of being mean" She said with a sad look on her face.

"That's not true Princess Khloe." Her father said walking from behind her.

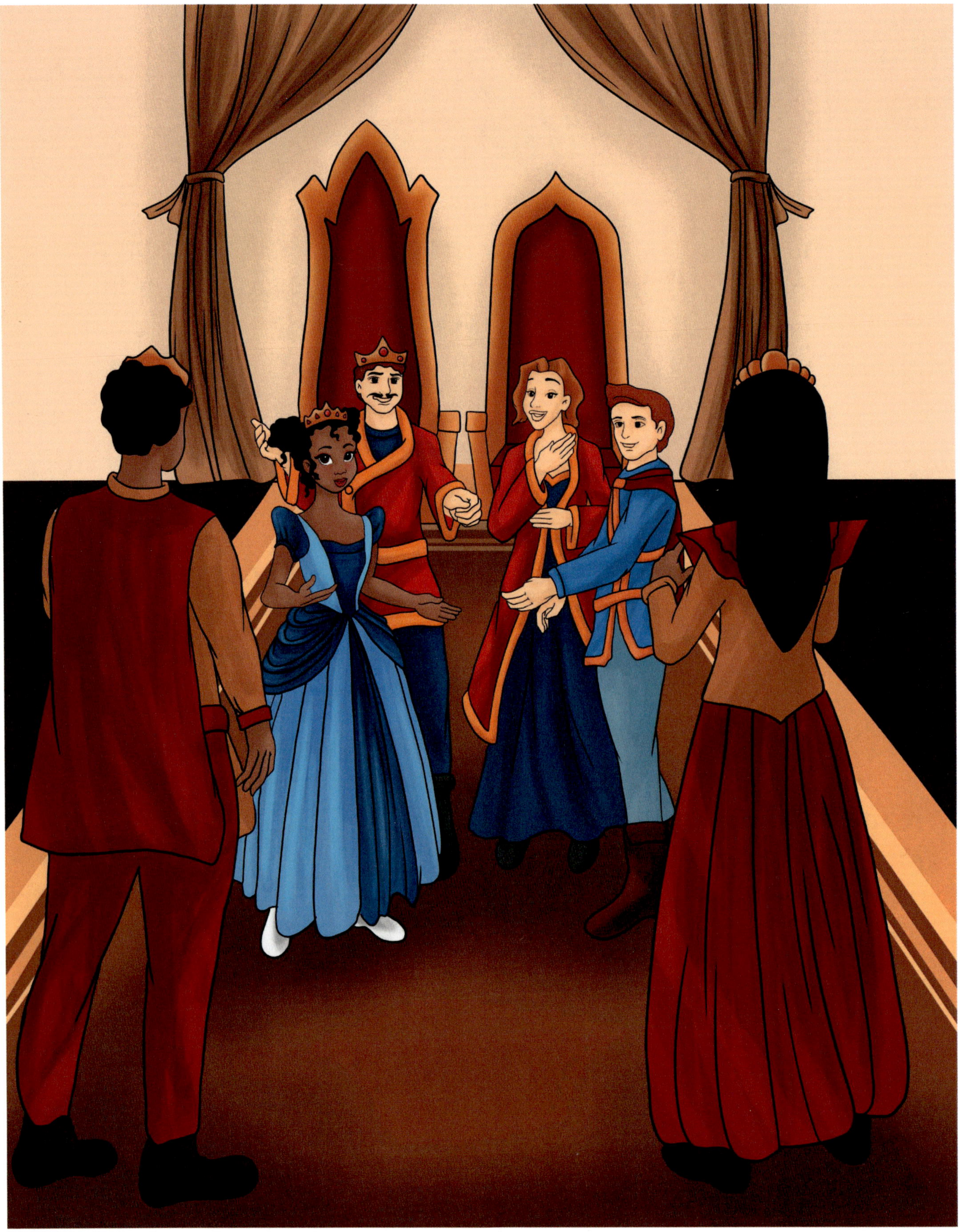

"No its not Princess." Her mother said walking behind him. "We were foolish to keep secrets from you and to keep you from being happy even if that meant you leaving the Badlands." Her mother told her.

"Your mother's right Princess. We hid you from the world when we knew you were different because we didn't want to lose you. Now that you're all grown you can make your own choices and we will respect that. We love you Princess and want you to be happy." He says beforeing kissing her forehead.

"So I can stay here in the Happy Lands?" She asked excitedly.

"Yes you can if it's ok with the King and Queen of the happy lands.

"Of course it is and I would like for us to end this ridiculousness for once and for all. Can't you see these children or even you and I really don't know what happened so many years ago between our two lands but it's affecting us and them. Say we call it truces?" The King of the happy lands says with his hand out.

"Truces." The King of the Badlands says before shaking the King of the Happy Lands hand.

Right then a course that hunted the two lands for many years was now broken because of the love of two teenagers. After five years of living in the Happy Lands Princess Khloe and Prince Ken went on to build their on land called the Land Of The Love Birds where they lived happily ever after.

THE END

◆ ◆ ◆

About The Author

Rasheed Latham

Hello everyone, my name is Rasheed Latham and I'm an author from Detroit, MI. This is my first children's book and it was inspired by my beautiful niece Khloe who is a princess in my eyes. I love you little lady.

Made in the USA
Columbia, SC
09 August 2022